What's the Big Idea, Molly?

Valeri Gorbachev

Philomel Books • An Imprint of Penguin Group (USA) Inc.

PATRICIA LEE GAUCH, EDITOR

PHILOMEL BOOKS
A division of Penguin Young Readers Group.
Published by The Penguin Group.
Penguin Group (USA) Inc., 375 Hudson Street, New York, NY 10014, U.S.A.
Penguin Group (Canada), 90 Eglinton Avenue East, Suite 700, Toronto, Ontario M4P 2Y3, Canada
(a division of Pearson Penguin Canada Inc.).
Penguin Books Ltd, 80 Strand, London WC2R 0RL, England.
Penguin Ireland, 25 St. Stephen's Green, Dublin 2, Ireland (a division of Penguin Books Ltd).
Penguin Group (Australia), 250 Camberwell Road, Camberwell, Victoria 3124, Australia
(a division of Pearson Australia Group Pty Ltd).
Penguin Books India Pvt Ltd, 11 Community Centre, Panchsheel Park, New Delhi - 110 017, India.
Penguin Group (NZ), 67 Apollo Drive, Rosedale, North Shore 0632, New Zealand
(a division of Pearson New Zealand Ltd).
Penguin Books (South Africa) (Pty) Ltd, 24 Sturdee Avenue, Rosebank, Johannesburg 2196, South Africa.
Penguin Books Ltd, Registered Offices: 80 Strand, London WC2R 0RL, England.

Design by Semadar Megged.   Text set in 15.5-point Galathea.
The illustrations are rendered in watercolors, gouache, and ink.

Library of Congress Cataloging-in-Publication Data
Gorbachev, Valeri.   What's the big idea, Molly? / Valeri Gorbachev.   p. cm.
Summary: Molly Mouse and her friends struggle to come up with ideas for birthday gifts for their
friend Turtle.   [1. Creative ability—Fiction. 2. Birthdays—Fiction. 3. Animals—Fiction.] I. Title.
PZ7.G6475Wf 2010   [E]—dc22   2009032337
ISBN 978-0-399-25428-4
Special Markets ISBN 978-0-399-25566-3 Not for resale
10 9 8 7 6 5 4 3

For Patti Gauch

Molly put down her notebook. It was not a good day for ideas. Molly had been trying to write a poem all morning—she loved beautiful words, but she just couldn't find an idea.

Now all her friends had come to Molly's house. Tomorrow was Turtle's ███████, but no one could come up with an idea for a gift for Turtle, either.

Molly put her pencil down.

"I know," Rabbit said. "A nice picture is a great ~~birthday~~ gift. I will draw a picture of a flower for Turtle."

"I like it," said Goose. "I will draw a picture of a flower for Turtle, too."

Frog jumped right off the couch. "Me, too. I love to draw flowers."

"And me," said Pig. "Flowers are my favorite things to draw."

"No, no, no," said Molly. "Drawing is a good idea, and I like to draw, too. But we can't give Turtle five pictures of a flower. We need to think."

"I think of my best ideas when I run," said Rabbit, walking out of the house.

"I think best when I am fishing!" Goose said, following him.

"I get my best ideas down by the pond," Frog said.

"Mine come to me under the willow tree," said Pig. "I'll be back soon."

"I am staying here," said Molly. "My best ideas come to me right here—when they come to me at all, that is."

And she sat down on the porch. Maybe she'd do better thinking up a gift for Turtle than she did thinking up a poem.

Meantime, Rabbit ran and ran and ran until he got the perfect new idea of what to draw for Turtle's ███████

Frog hopped to the pond
and plopped in.

He swam and swam until he got a great idea of
what to draw for Turtle's birthday.

Goose waddled down to the lake.

He fished and fished until he got just the right idea
of what to draw for Turtle's ███████

Pig went right to the willow tree. And she took a nap!
That's how she got her best ideas.

When she woke up, she knew just what to draw.

When all the friends ran to Molly's house with
their new ideas, Molly still had no idea at all!
"What ideas did you come up with?" she asked,
a bit grumpy.

"Running through the woods, I saw a beautiful tree. I am drawing the tree for Turtle," said Rabbit.
"I am sure Turtle will love it."

"Oh, dear," said Frog. "Jumping into the pond, I saw a beautiful tree, too. Two pictures of trees will be all right, won't they?"

"You will not believe it," said Goose, "but I caught a fish under a most beautiful tree as well, and I have drawn that very tree for Turtle. Three very good pictures of trees will be all right, too. . . . Right?"

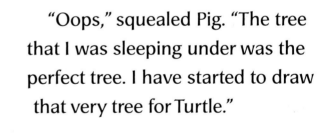

"Oops," squealed Pig. "The tree that I was sleeping under was the perfect tree. I have started to draw that very tree for Turtle."

"Oh, goodness," said Molly. "First it was all flowers, now it is all trees! You can't all give Turtle a picture of a tree . . . hmmm. Wait, I've got an idea!"

She sat down on the porch with her pad and pencil and began to write.

"What is it, Molly?" said her friends. "Do you want to draw a tree, too?"

"No," said Molly, without looking up. "Just wait, please."

Then Molly told everyone her idea and they all loved it.

Molly and her friends got busy working on Turtle's present together.

They drew and painted and glued and stapled until it was finished.

The next day was Turtle's ████████. They met him down by the pond and sang "████████████" to him, then all together gave him one—just one— wrapped present.

It was a beautiful book from his five friends, with beautiful pictures for every season.

The summer picture was drawn by Rabbit.

Summer

In summer
It's so hot
I feel like I'm
In a melting pot

Goose drew the autumn picture.

Autumn

Fall is in the air
Leaves are blowing
Here and there

Frog drew the winter picture.

Winter

Snow
Is crystal white
It shines
In the night

Pig, who loved spring best, drew spring.

Spring

Spring is here
Let's give a cheer
It's the best season
Of the year

And Molly wrote every beautiful word.

"I love this book," said Turtle. "And I love all of you. I will think of you whenever I read it."

And they all sat down and had a great ██████, party together.

When Molly went home, she sat back on the porch step.
"I wonder," she said, picking up her notebook and pencil,
"if I will get another big idea tomorrow."

"I am ready for it."